D4J

From the authorized animated series
based on the original tales

BY **BEATRIX POTTER**™

F. WARNE & Cº

Once upon a time there was an old tailor who lived in Gloucester.

He sat in his little shop in Westgate Street, cross-legged on
a table, working from morning till night.

3

One bitter cold day near Christmas, the tailor began to make a coat; a coat of cherry-coloured corded silk.

'The finest of wedding coats for the Mayor of Gloucester who is to be married on Christmas Day in the morning,' he muttered.

The table was littered with snippets of the rich cherry-coloured silk and exquisite yellow taffeta.

'I'm sure I cannot afford to waste the smallest piece,' said
the tailor as he continued cutting. 'Too narrow breadths
for nought except waistcoats for mice!'

Unnoticed, little mice retrieved the scraps from his work bench and carried them off.

'I cannot remember when we had silk of such quality on these premises!' exclaimed the little mouse.

'The light is fading and I am tired. All is ready to sew in the morning, except for one item – I am wanting one single skein of cherry-coloured twisted silk thread.'

The old tailor locked up his shop and headed for home through the snow.

The mice were more fortunate and did not have to brave
the cold. With their secret passages they could run all over
town, from house to house, without ever going out into the
streets.

The tailor lived alone with his cat, Simpkin, who kept
house while the tailor worked. Simpkin was *very* fond of
mice but he gave them no satin for coats!

'Ah, Simpkin, old friend!' exclaimed the tailor as he arrived home. 'We shall make our fortune, but I am worn to a ravelling. Take this groat (which is our last fourpence) and buy a penn'orth of bread, a penn'orth of milk and a penn'orth of sausages.'

'And oh, Simpkin,' remembered the tailor, 'with the last penny of our fourpence buy me a penn'orth of cherry-coloured silk. But do not lose the last penny, Simpkin, for I have *no more twist*.'

Weary from his day's work, the tailor sat by the fire and began to dream about that beautiful coat.

Suddenly his thoughts were interrupted by little noises coming from the dresser - *Tip tap, tip tap tip*!

He crossed the kitchen and stood quite still beside the dresser, listening carefully.

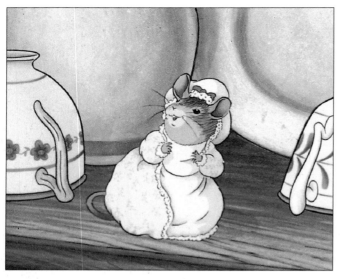

Tip tap, tip tap, tip tap tip!
    The tailor lifted up a teacup. Out stepped a live lady mouse. Then, from under the teacups, bowls and basins, stepped more and more little mice!

'This is very peculiar,' remarked the tailor. 'I'll wager this
is all Simpkin's doing, the rascal.

'Oh, was I wise to entrust my last fourpence to
Simpkin? And was it right to let loose those mice?'

Simpkin returned and opened the door with an angry
'G-r-r-miaw!' for he hated the snow. He looked
suspiciously at the dresser – the cups and jugs had been
moved!

'Simpkin,' asked the tailor anxiously, 'where is my twist?'

'Where is my mouse?' wondered Simpkin and quickly hid the twist in the teapot.

'Alack, I am undone,' lamented the tailor and went sadly to bed.

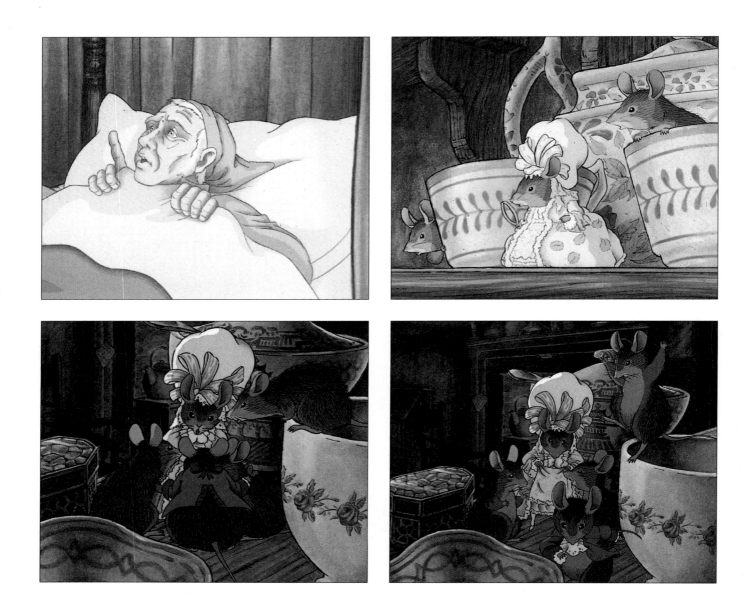

The poor old tailor was ill with fever. Tossing and turning in his bed he mumbled, 'No more twist . . . one-and-twenty buttonholes . . . to be finished by noon on Saturday . . . and it is already Tuesday!'

Indeed, what should become of the cherry-coloured coat?

In the tailor's shop the embroidered silk and satin lay ready and cut out on the table, but who should come to sew them when the window was barred and the door locked?

The tailor lay ill for three days and three nights and then it was Christmas Eve. The moon climbed up over the roofs and chimneys. All the city of Gloucester was fast asleep under the snow.

The cathedral clock struck twelve and Simpkin went out
into the night.

For an old story tells of how all the animals can talk in the night between Christmas Eve and Christmas Day in the morning (though very few people can hear them).

Simpkin wandered through the streets but when he turned
a corner he saw a glow of light coming from his master's
shop. He crept up to the window to peep in.

Inside the shop was a snippeting of scissors and a
snappeting of thread and little mouse voices were singing
loudly and happily:
  'Three little mice sat down to spin,
  Pussy passed by and she peeped in . . .'

Simpkin miaowed to get in but the door was locked and
the key under the tailor's pillow.

He came away from the shop and made his way home.
There he found the tailor, without fever and sleeping
peacefully.

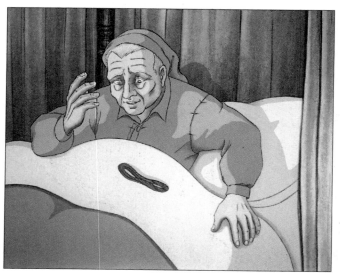

Simpkin felt very ashamed after seeing those good little mice. He took the silk from the teapot and placed it on his master's bed.

'Alack, I am worn to a ravelling, but I have my twist,' said the Tailor of Gloucester.

The next morning the tailor went out into the street and made his way to his shop.

'I have my twist,' he said, 'but no more strength or time for this is Christmas Day in the morning.' He opened the door and looked in amazement.

Upon the table – oh joy! There, where he had left plain cuttings of silk lay the most beautiful coat and satin waistcoat!

Everything was finished except one single cherry-coloured buttonhole, where there was pinned a scrap of paper with these teeny weeny words – NO MORE TWIST.

From then began the luck of the Tailor of Gloucester.
Never were seen such ruffles and embroidered cuffs. But his
buttonholes were the greatest triumph – the stitches were *so*
neat and *so* small they looked as if they had been made by
little mice!